DAVE

SUE HENDRA

Illustrated by Liz Pichon

Hodder Children's Books

A division of Hachette Children's Books

Dave
was
BIG...

DAVE

by Sue Hendra
Illustrated by Liz Pichon
First published in 2009 by
Hodder Children's Books
This paperback edition
published in 2010

Hodder Children's Books
338 Euston Road
London, NW1 3 BH

Hodder Children's Books Australia
Level 17/207 Kent Street
Sydney, NSW 2000

ISBN: 978 0 340 97037 9
10 9 8 7 6 5 4 3 2 1

Printed in China

Hodder Children's Books is a division of Hachette Children's Books.
An Hachette UK Company.

www.hachette.co.uk

To LiLY

For Paul, and for Clive
for adding the parp S.H

...and
quite
fantastic.

And so were his dinners!

After an enormous breakfast,
Dave headed outside for a
snooze in the sun.

He pushed his head through
the cat flap and placed one
paw in front of the other,
but he couldn't move!

Dave was...

...STUCK!

'Hi there,'
sniggered a bug.

'You'll never guess
what's happened
to Dave,' the bug
whispered to
the dog.
'He's stuck!'

The dog told the caterpillar.

The caterpillar told the birds.

The birds told the squirrels.

The squirrels told the hedgehog, and soon everyone in the garden knew!

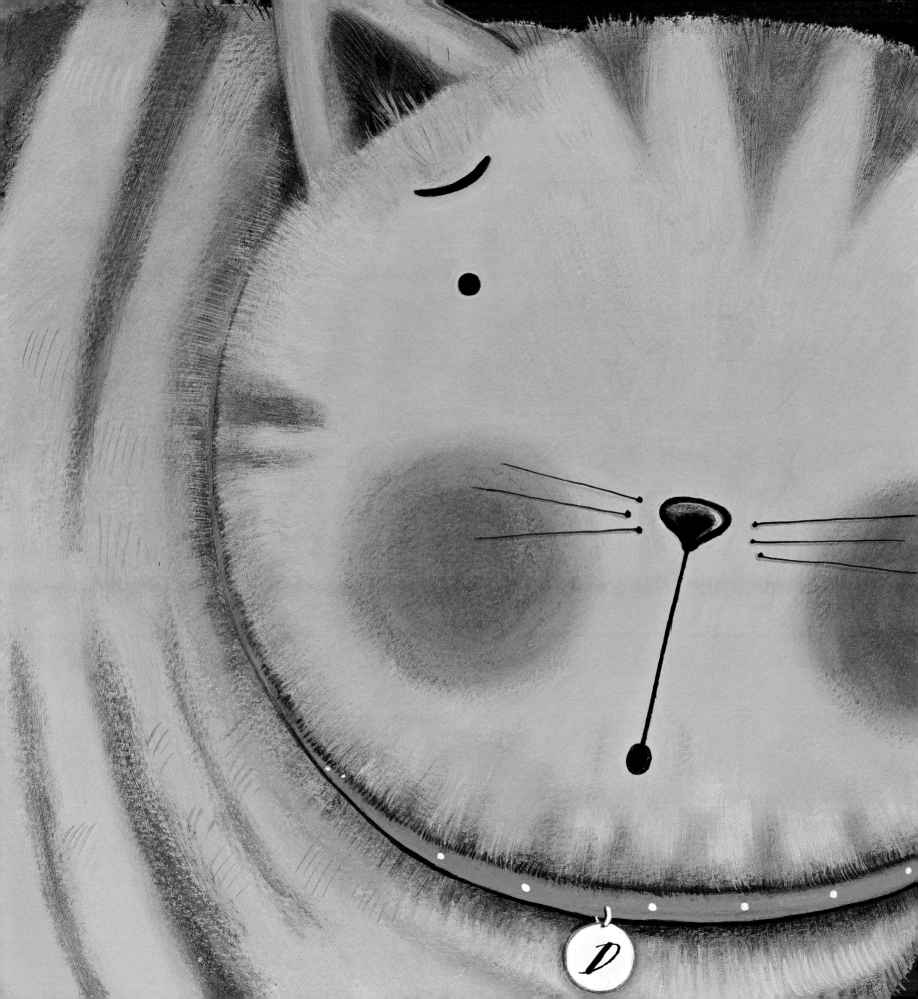

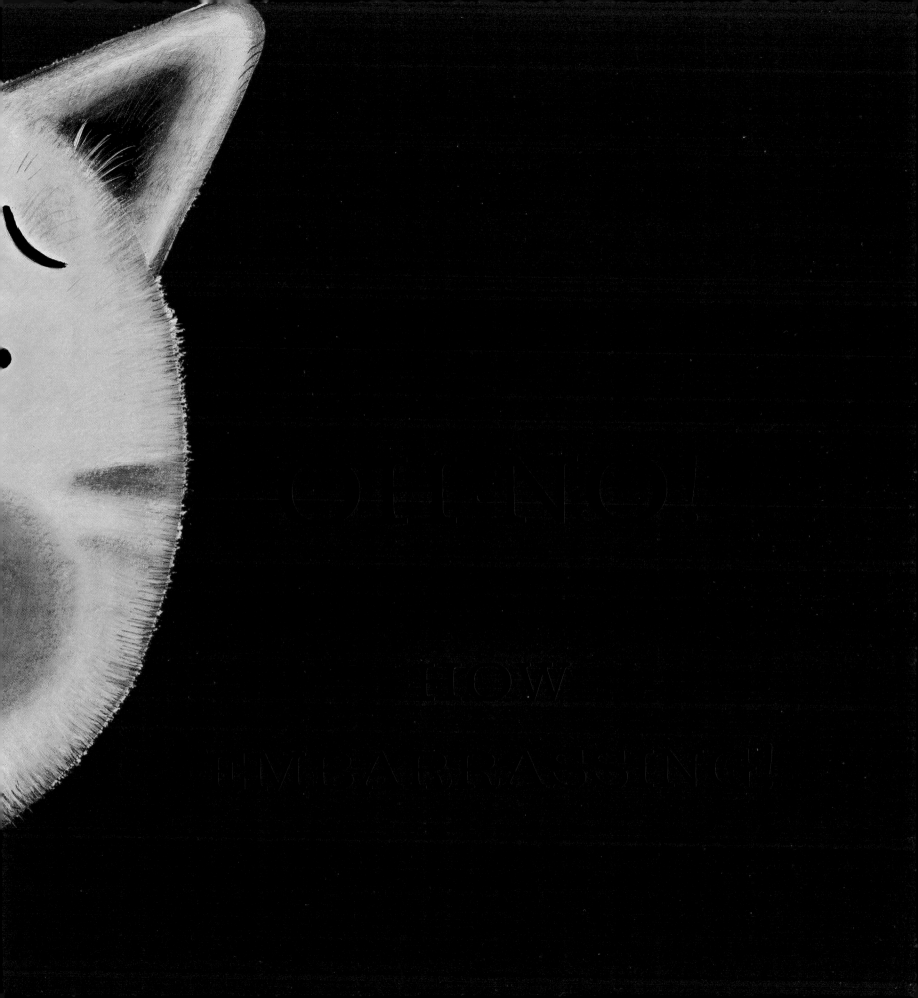

OH NO!

HOW

EMBARRASSING!

The animals got together
and decided to help
set Dave free.

Dog thought he could
scare him free.

WOOOF!

And Dave
was scared.

AARGH!!!

But he was also still stuck.

The animals wondered if they could tempt Dave out with tasty treats.

Yum! Yum!

Yum! Yum!

But worms were definitely
not Dave's idea of a tasty treat.

They even tried to tickle
Dave out!

Hee! Hee!

Hee! Hee!

But it was no good.
He was still stuck.

Suddenly the bug had a bright idea...

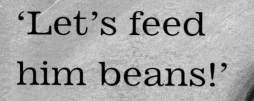

'Let's feed him beans!'

It was a strange plan.
But Dave opened his mouth
wide as the animals catapulted
beans into it one after another.

Dave liked this game A LOT.

Dave
caught
more beans...

And
more
beans...

And more beans...

Until...

Dave shook. The ground shook.
Something very big was about
to happen...

5 4 3 2 1

BLAST

OFF!

It was a long walk home for Dave, but when he finally got there...

A LONG WAY TO GO →

...boy was he hungry!